The Secret lives of Monsters and Legends

Re-imagined by
Sunny & Ben

First Printing, 2015

ISBN 978-1-68222-354-3

Sunny & Ben Books
34 Gilbert House
Churchill Gardens
Pimlico, London.
SW1V 3HN

www.SunnyandBenBooks.com

Dedication.

This book is dedicated to my niece, Sienna, and to all the curious, imaginative and fun loving children all over the world just like her.

You have it in you to become whatever you dream of, so please do not let the 'monsters' of this world tell you otherwise. Learn, believe and achieve!

- Sunny Basra

Acknowledgments.

There are those whos advice and support can make or break a project, and this book could not have been finished without the following people;

Mr G J Adams, Jordan Crawley, Fabio Gangarossa, and Carol Gangarossa, Claire Lawrence, Emma Lawrence, Nisha Mahay, Annie Meszaros, Raji Rai, Sam Stratford, Jade Warriner-Doyle, and Carol Warriner-Doyle for all your unwaivering support with proofreading and your invaluable feedback. In addition, we would like to say thank you to our friends for unwillingly lending me their names. (Sunny speaks) My mother, Rani Basra, also needs a special mention, as well as close family and friends, for each of you have had an impact on me at some stage, and have helped to shape the moral fabric of the man I am today.

Most importantly however, is to say thank you to our little star's who read this book and gave us the thumbs-up! Alisha, Ava, Ellie, Sienna and Summer; Your opinions mattered to us greatly, and without your blessings, this book wouldn't be where it is now – complete!

Lastly, Ben and I would like to thank Jake, Janic and the team at BookBaby for providing their assistance, for their patience (which was solidly tested!) and for the brilliant and uncompromising platform upon which this book was given life. We'll try to make it easier for you guy's next time, but no promises!

Let's Connect!

Join us on Facebook for latest news and offers! Just search for SunnyandBenBooks

Keep up to date and share your thoughts on Twitter! Lookup @sunnybenbooks

To show our appreciation, we have a gift for you! Visit us at www.sunnyandbenbooks.com to let us know what you thought of our book, and you will receive your exclusive Monsters & Legends wallpaper!

Contents List

Chapter 1.

Out in the woods, in the darkest depths, there are stories of a scary monster that lives there. He is known as Bigfoot. The people all over the world have heard about this creature, yet have never seen it. "How does he live" and "does he have any friends" the people have asked. No person has ever been able to answer these questions. So if no person knows anything about Bigfoot,  how can people still think that he is scary and dangerous?

This is just one question a young adventurer named Carl was eager to answer. To Carl, Bigfoot was a mystery, and as such it needed to be solved. This was a challenge that Carl really wanted to take on. Was Carl scared? Yes he was! However, Carl had been taught that being scared was OK, and that it was good to face your fears.

Through the years Carl had heard people talk about Bigfoot. They would say that the monster was big, and hairy, and scary! This made Carl even more intrigued. Did the people make this up or was there some truth in this? Carl asked many people, young and old, and they all said the same thing: "If you see Bigfoot, don't look, RUN!" (Carl thought this was silly, as you should always look when you run!). Other people from the surrounding towns said that the story was made up, and Bigfoot didn't even exist! "This doesn't seem fair!" said Carl out aloud. Clearly Carl didn't like people calling Bigfoot names and making up stories about him being a "Monster" and so became his new mission! His inner adventurer was even more determined than ever to find Bigfoot so that he, and the whole world, would know the truth!

Chapter 2

Today was the day to find Bigfoot, and Carl was ready, but he knew it wouldn't be easy! The challenge ahead reminded Carl of the other stories he'd heard. One man had told him "whenever Bigfoot is seen, he can hide like a mouse" and another once said "Bigfoot is so fast that he can beat a cheetah". Carl thought about all the stories and realized he needed a different approach, and so it was time to go. It was early morning, and Carl had just finished packing his backpack. He went through his checklist; Sandwiches and water "check", Torch "Check", Map "check", and mobile phone "check". This was it, somehow, some way, Carl would meet Bigfoot today!!

The day was warm and humid, the sunlight trickling through the treetops. As Carl scampered through the thick undergrowth of the forest, many thoughts were racing through his mind. Would he be able to find Bigfoot at all, and if he did, how would he get away if the Bigfoot were the nasty creature everyone said he was? This reminded Carl of a lesson he was taught by his Granddad "some people are scared of things they do not understand." This gave Carl a touch of confidence in his meeting with Bigfoot, knowing that he would be able to judge for himself.

Carl was getting tired; moving through the forest was hard. It was time for a break. Carl spotted a fallen tree in a small clearing. He sat, and began to enjoy the tasty sandwiches he had prepared. He began to ponder about what it might be like to live in this forest, just like Bigfoot. What might he eat? How

and where does he sleep? As he finished his sandwiches he noticed that it was getting dark, soon he would not be able to see through the forest. Should he camp here, or turn back now? There had been no signs of the creature, would he even find him? Was he even real? As he was sitting there on the fallen tree, unsure of what to do, he decided to look again at his map and compass, surely this would help him decide. As he carefully studied the map, he realised that he had checked all the area's where people had claimed they had seen Bigfoot. "This isn't helping me at all!" Carl said to himself.

As he stared aimlessly at the map, Carl spotted something at the corner of his eye that made him freeze! Was it real? He couldn't believe it; he had to take a closer look. Right there, just beside the fallen tree, covered by a layer of stray leaves was the biggest footprint he'd ever seen! It was at least twice the size of any man's foot, yet amazingly had all five toes. "Was Bigfoot an overgrown man?" Carl whispered to himself. Carl's scouts training kicked in, he had experience of tracking from his childhood, and he'd been the best tracker in his scout group. Carl noticed the footprint was still moist and soft. This meant the Bigfoot had been here recently, and could possibly be quite near. This gave Carl the Goosebumps; there was now a real possibility of meeting the elusive Bigfoot. He'd found the first clue, and it had been there right next to him all that time!

There was no time for resting, it was time to finally prove all the stories and claim his glory!

Chapter 3

The footprints were leading Carl in a different direction. As he looked at his map, he noticed that he was walking into an uncharted area of the forest, far away from where people had spotted him. "He was certainly good at hiding" Carl said to himself, smirking to himself as he thought of how well Bigfoot

had evaded humans. It was getting dark, and still there was no sign of Bigfoot. Still, the fresh footprints were giving Carl real hope. Sooner or later, he would find the creature.

As Carl was struggling through the forest, now thicker and tougher than he'd ever experienced he spotted something ahead that sent shivers down his spine. He could just make out a large, dark silhouette through the bushes. Was he imagining this or was it real? Carl couldn't move, he was fixed to the spot. His heart was beating faster than ever before; he was

both scared and excited, as he couldn't believe what his eyes were seeing. The shape was motionless, had the creature spotted Carl? There was just enough light to make out that this was like no creature Carl had ever seen. He knew that if this was real, he'd made the biggest discovery ever!

Slowly, Carl edged forward, trying to be as quiet as possible. The creature was doing something, but what could it be? Can you guess what it is? This was the closest anyone had ever been to the Bigfoot, Carl had to be very cautious, and move slowly so he didn't startle or scare it away. "My-oh-my, this is so exciting" Carl ushered; life couldn't get better than this for an adventurer. At that moment, Carl thought of how he would call for help if he got into trouble. The mobile phone was useless now as he was too far into the forest, and shouting would not work as nobody was around for miles. There was no time for negative thoughts, Carl had come too far and this would be his moment of triumph, be what may. This would be the first time ever that anybody had seen Bigfoot alive, and in action! Ok, here we go, this is it, the time to finally see what the mystery is about...

Carl slowly parted the branches of the tree's to get a better look. As he carefully moved the last branch that blocked his view, he knew that what he was seeing was absolutely impossible to believe; yet there it was! Carl was in utter shock.

In a cleared space, right in the middle of this dense forest, was the Bigfoot, sat at a computer, hard at work? Carl really couldn't believe what he was seeing. It was definitely the Bigfoot, but not as he had imagined it would be. Was he imagining things himself? Was he really seeing this happen? As he gazed in disbelief, the Bigfoot slowly turned his head, smiled, and in a soft, kind voice said, "Hello Carl, how was your journey?" Carl almost fainted, he couldn't speak, he couldn't move. After a few moments, Carl tried to speak. "H-h-h-hello" he murmured, in a quiet, croaky voice. The Bigfoot slowly stood up, and reached out his hand to shake Carl's. He was much bigger, and hairier than Carl ever imagine. He had a warm smile, round spectacles and spoke perfect English just like Carl's Granddad. Finally, Carl began to relax, and could feel his legs again. He slowly reached out his hand, and gave an awkward smile. "Hi, my name is Sasquatch...but you'll know me as Bigfoot" said the creature. Carl nodded, still unable to speak properly. He began to think, why couldn't this be true? Sasquatch was like any other creature, except he could speak and use computers! How did he even get a computer to work here? Ignoring the most obvious questions, Carl gave in and decided he would just believe. There had been many times in history when people had not believed and yet things had become true. Can you think of any examples? Sasquatch offered Carl a seat, and sat beside him. Carl kindly accepted and finally managed to say something: "Thank you Sasquatch," he said, sounding more comfortable and confident. Carl knew that this moment would probably never come again, so took his opportunity to ask Sasquatch another question. "Sasquatch, why do you run away when people see you? Why do you not stand and speak to humans?" Sasquatch sighed and looked upset. He knew Carl was not like other humans, so decided to show him his work and let him into his secret.

Sasquatch opened a tab on his Internet browser and showed the young adventurer a page on the screen. "Look at this Carl, this show's you how humans have behaved in the past. There are many things that humans do not understand, and as your Granddad told you, humans are often scared of things they do not understand. And when they are scared, they react in silly ways. They have harmed animals and creatures of the world in the past, many driven to extinction." As Sasquatch explained,

Carl understood why Sasquatch had been hiding. Ignoring how on earth Sasquatch knew what his Granddad had told him (at this point ANYTHING could be true!) Carl asked another question: "So what do you do when the humans are not bothering you?" Sasquatch smiled, and showed Carl another page. "You see Carl, humans have lost their connection with nature, and that's a real shame. Not all humans are the same, some are kind and understanding like you. I help all the animals of the world keep connected so that we can keep them safe and living happily together, but sadly I cannot help them all. That is why it is very important to have kind humans like you to help take care of nature, and protect endangered species, both animals and plants. If every person in the world could do this, I would be able to retire just like your Granddad!" Carl smiled, because he had just realized something very profound. Sasquatch had just taught him that if we all do our own part in helping to protect our environment and the species within it, slowly but surely, humans could re-connect with nature and help the world get better, rather than destroy it.

As a bonus, Carl also learnt something else. Even though Sasquatch was a creature, he had a personality, he was living and breathing and as such should be treated with respect. He was no different from any human in the world. Carl decided that he would not take a photo of Sasquatch, or tell anybody he actually existed, as he deserved his privacy. Nobody needed to know where he lived however they did need to hear his message.

Humans were not ready; they did not need to meet Sasquatch yet because they had even more important things to do, which was to learn to love each other and nature, and begin repairing the damage they had done. Carl promised Sasquatch that he would try to help people understand this, and that one day, his work could be complete so he could finally retire and enjoy his life!

The end.

Chapter 1.

Up in the foothills of the Carpathian Mountains was a place called Transylvania, in Romania. In Transylvania there was a very old castle. In that castle lived a vampire named Count Dracula. He was thought to be the scariest of all the monsters and was older than the castle itself. Dracula lived alone, and was rumoured to be immortal. He looked like a human, but he was definitely different. Nobody knew him or ever saw him, however they could see the shape of a man in the window

when the lightening would strike, and the thunder would crack.

The legends would tell that he had big fangs, greenish skin with slick black hair, and he wore a shiny black cape. It was not known if he had any family or friends. The people in the surrounding towns never, ever ventured to that castle. They had heard terrible stories, but nobody knew what was true and what was false … they never went there because they were too scared.

The castle lay at the top of a hill, above the village of Arefu. In this small village, lived a young girl called Sienna. Her mother would tell the stories of Dracula, and warned her never to go near the castle. Sienna would listen, and every night promised her mother that she would never go near the castle.

One stormy night, when Sienna had been tucked into bed, she saw something that would change her for life! As she lay in her bed, the thunder was deafening with lightning flashing bright, and reaching farther than the eye could see. Just then, a flash from the skies illuminated the castle, showing her a large manly figure in the window! This was the first time ever Sienna had seen anyone in that castle, and she just couldn't believe it. She had a curious nature that was beginning to overwhelm her. Sienna didn't know it yet, but she was about to do a terrible thing. On this night, she was about to break the promise she had given to her mother, and would walk up to the castle to take a closer look.

Brave and determined, Sienna walked out of the house and began her trek up the hill towards Dracula's Castle. As she walked up the muddy path, Sienna began to remember the stories her Mother would tell her every night. "Dracula is bad," her mother would say. Despite this, Sienna could not turn back; she had to see what Dracula was for herself.

Chapter 2.

Sienna was an inquisitive, and very friendly child. She had a cheeky and fun nature, and was always able to make friends easily. As her mother had said many times, Dracula lived alone. That night, seeing just the one figure in the window, Sienna began to wonder whether this was true. With this in mind, and being as nice as she was, Sienna had decided to take some sweets with her as a gift for Dracula.

The thunder and lightening was now far into the distance, the night had become eerily still. Sienna was now right up at the foot of the castle itself. She looked up and could see a big man with pointy ears standing with his back to the window. There

was definitely someone there! Was that Dracula himself? Sienna was excited, she had no idea who or what she would meet inside.

At the entrance was an old, metal door with a big iron knocker, it looked heavy she thought. She gave it 2 loud knocks. The castle was big and scary looking with spider webs covering every corner, and bats hanging from the surrounding trees. Yes, this place was really dark, but the young girl was not afraid. She waited and waited, and nothing happened. Suddenly, the door creaked opened slowly by itself, she looked up at the window and the figure was still there.

Sienna stepped into the castle, peered round the door to find nobody there. Ahead of her was a spiral staircase that went as high as the eye could see. This castle was bigger than she had hought! There were no other doors, just the stairs. What a funny castle she thought, "who doesn't have any downstairs rooms?" she said to herself as she chuckled to herself. Sienna began to walk up the stairs, each step echoed through the vast tower as she slowly went up, and the stairs seeming to go up forever. It was dark, only lit by the open flame torches that hung from the bare stonewalls. Sienna knew what to do, she had been told by her mother not to play with fire, but she needed the torch to see the step. She held it carefully by the handle, as she continued up and up and up.

Finally, Sienna arrived at the landing. Ahead of her was a single room, and that was all. How odd she thought! Only one room in a big castle like this, what was the point?

She could see a flicker of light coming from the room. She tiptoed, getting closer. There was a lovely warmth coming from inside the room, and she could hearing the crackling of an open fire. Sienna loved open fires, as they were so cosy!

Finally she would be able to see Dracula, and hopefully find out what all the stories were about. She slowly pushed open the door to look inside…

Chapter 3

"Noooo!" boomed a voice from inside. This startled Sienna, who fell back out on the landing. Oh "What's the matter with you?" she shouted back, as she dusted herself off, "don't you know it's rude to shout at a guest?" Sienna quickly stood up, stormed towards the room and pushed open the door, ready to confront the person inside… and to find a most surprising sight. It was Dracula!! With a teddy bear? The young girl, sweets in hand, was speechless. It was rare for her not to know what to say. This was definitely the strangest thing she'd ever seen. The 'man' looked just like her mum had explained. He had long pointy ears, greenish skin and a cape, but that was all the resemblance she could make out. There was nothing scary or evil about this Dracula at all. In fact, he looked like a scared little boy. He was sucking his thumb and holding onto his teddy bear. Even Sienna didn't suck her thumbs anymore! "Are you ok?" asked Sienna. She had quickly forgotten his rude greeting, and was more concerned than anything. Sienna was a smart girl, and she knew when somebody looked down.

She offered Dracula the sweets. "Why are you being nice to me?" asked Dracula. "That's because I'm a nice person" she

replied, with a beaming smile. Dracula seemed nervous, but after a moment he accepted the sweets and smiled back at Sienna. This was the first time anybody had been nice to him. Sienna was happy to be the first one, but was sad because she realised that people had mistaken Dracula for a mean monster. She could see that Dracula was friendly, yet sadly was all alone. Sienna sat beside him, she was determined to help Dracula, and felt like she could be his friend. "Why are you here alone?" she asked him.

Dracula thought about her question for a moment, hesitant to reply. "I won't laugh, you can tell me," she said reassuringly. Dracula could feel that Sienna was being nice for real, she was genuine, so he plucked the courage to answer her question. "I'm afraid, I'm afraid that

nobody will like me," he said. Sienna, being the person she was, immediately knew what to do. She had learnt from her mother that helping a sad person was one of the kindest things a person could do, and helping the person to understand that they were not the only person who felt that way was a gift that money could not buy. "I know how you feel Count Dracula, I too have felt afraid for the same reason, yet look at me, I have many friends, and you can be one of them!" Dracula could not help but to feel ecstatic with joy. "Really, he said, you promise?" "Of course" she replied, "I promise". Just then she remembered something one of her own friends had told her when she was once feeling sad. "Don't let yourself, get yourself down – my friend Milo told me that!" Dracula stopped for a moment to think about that. He understood what she meant, and leapt up in excitement! "I will not let myself get myself down!" he said proudly. "Now you have to promise me something!" said Dracula. "I want you to promise me that you will not disobey your mother! She asked you to never come her and you did exactly that." Sienna knew that Dracula was right and agreed immediately that she would not do that again. As they shook hands and made their promises, Dracula stood up.

"Would you like to see a neat trick?" he asked in excitement. "Yes of course" she said, "what is it?" In a blink of an eye, Dracula transformed into a bat and began to fly around the room. "Very impressive" she said as she applauded his flying skills.

Sienna had always felt that Dracula was innocent of all the bad rumours about him, and this made her think that not everything you hear about a person is true. You should always try to meet them for yourself, and be nice, and then you can make up your own mind. Count Dracula was just like any other person, a friendly vampire who just wanted some friends. She was now his first ever friend, and it made them both happy!

The end.

GEORGE AND THE DRAGON

Chapter One

Long ago, there was a land where brave knights in armour protected the people of the villages and small towns. They would protect against invaders from distant lands across the oceans. However, these invaders were not always from distant lands, and they were not always human. DRAGONS! These were giant flying monsters that ruled the skies and everything under them. Many stories had been told of fire breathing dragons that ruined villages and destroyed towns in search of

food and treasures. The only protection the people had were the brave knights of the realm.

In the largest of these town lived a knight called George. He was the bravest of all the knights. All the people in the land loved George for his mighty strength and skills as a knight. They loved him because he was their most fierce soldier. He had led armies against invaders from far away lands, and this knight would always win his battles. Even greater than beating armies, he was the best at beating dragons, and for this he became known as a living legend. However, even though they loved the legend, nobody really knew him. Those who had been lucky to meet him told stories of George being a mean and moody man. They thought he was such a good fighter that they didn't care if he was an angry knight, and most people were too scared to even talk to him because of the stories they had heard. As long as he protected them, they did not care what he was like. Was this fair to George?

One thing that made George such a great knight is that he never let the dragon get close to the town. His battles with the dragon were always far away, which of course made the people very happy. The dragon would fly past, the sky watchers would ring the warning bell and upon hearing it George would jump onto his faithful horse, and chase after the dragon into the distance. They always knew that George was out there battling to protect them from the dragon. No other knight was a true match for this dragon, except of course for George!

One evening, George was preparing supper for Charlie, his new horse, when the sky watchers sounded the warning bell. This could only mean they had spotted the dragon high in the sky, and were quick to raise the alarm. The dragon swooped down and flew close to the rooftops of the town houses. George was as quick as lightning! He was always ready to go into battle. He leapt onto his horse and they galloped towards the dragon. George pulled out his long sharp sword and began to scream and shout as he charged towards the dragon. The dragon was

of course in the sky, so how would George be able to do anything? Despite this, the dragon was still scared off and began to flee towards the wooded mountains. George galloped behind him, sword in hand and braver than ever.

"Freddie, We're lucky that this dragon never has a chance to breath his fire," said one sky watcher to the other. "You shouldn't believe in luck Tom," replied Freddie, "we made our own luck by warning George early enough, so that he protect us." The two nodded in agreement as they saw George and Charlie chase after the dragon into the wooded mountain.

In the wooded mountain, hidden within the thick bush was a deep, dark cave. Inside the cave is where the dragon lived. How did George know this? Surely he must have had many battles with the Dragon there?

On that day George followed the dragon to that cave. The cave was in the darkest part of the mountain, where it was spooky and mysterious. Charlie did not like to be left outside the cave, however, he knew George was doing this for his own protection. George and Charlie waited outside the cave quietly,

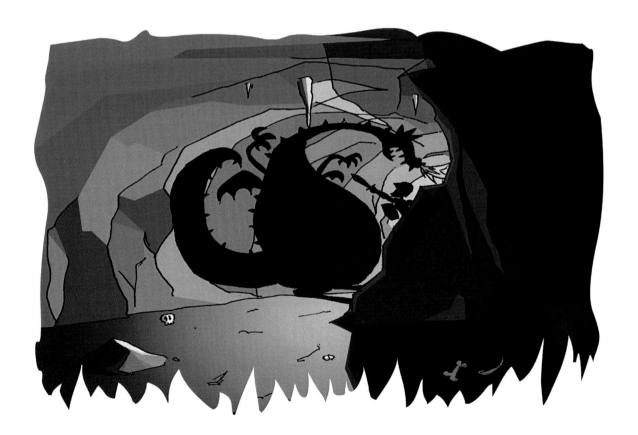

trying to see if they could hear what the dragon was doing. The dragon was making some odd noises in there, it sound like he was moving furniture? "This is too strange" said Charlie, and decided he would definitely stay outside, while George went in to investigate. George entered the dark cave to see what the dragon was doing.

After some moments in the dark cave, there was a sudden flash of bright flame followed by a huge roar! This frightened Charlie very much, as he could see George and the Dragon's shadow, with George's sword drawn and aiming at the dragon! "Has the fight started?" said Charlie to himself as he took cover.

Meanwhile, inside the cave, something totally unexpected was happening. It was dark, and the cave had become totally silent. The dragon was no longer making any sounds. George had crept through the cave, one careful step at a time, not knowing where the dragon was. As he came to the end of the passage in the cave...

Chapter 3

"SURPRISE!!" shouted the dragon. What was happening here? The dragon had a cake with candles, presents and toys set up, all for George! Why? It was George's birthday today. George could not believe that the dragon had remembered. "Thank you so much Seref!" exclaimed George, "you really are a true friend!" Could this be true, that George and Seref the Dragon are actually friends?

Outside, Charlie was waiting, and was beginning to wonder what was happening in the cave. The sounds coming from inside the cave were like laughter, not fighting! He decided he would go into the cave to investigate. Charlie trotted to the end of the passage and peered around the corner and could not believe what he was seeing! Charlie was confused by what he was seeing. He was also upset at George for leaving him outside! "You're having fun without me?" said Charlie. "Oh bless you Charlie," replied George, "I'm so sorry, come here and sit with us, and let me explain to you what is going on while we enjoy some cake."

As Charlie enjoyed the cake, he listened carefully to George's story. "We have been friends for many years", said George. "Long ago, I rescued Seref from a horrible mob who wanted to hurt him". "Why were they trying to hurt him?" asked Charlie. "They had been attacked by a dragon", George explained, and thought it was Seref. Instead of hearing what Seref had to say, they began to attack him. They did not give him the chance to explain. They had the wrong dragon! So instead of battling Seref, I drew him away from the mad crowd, and bought him to this cave so he could make a new home where he would be safe."

"George was so kind to me," Seref added. He had a reputation for being a nasty knight, be he really wasn't. So to say thank you, I would celebrate his birthday with him every year because nobody else was as close to him" Seref continued to explain. "Every year I would fly over the town, just as I did today, so that the people ring the warning bell. That way George would know I am there and he would follow me on his horse into the wooded mountain to my home.

"Seref is not a mean dragon like people think he is" said George. Charlie nodded as he heard the story, and began to understand why Seref never breathed fire onto the town or harmed any of the people there. This story taught Charlie two important lessons.

Firstly, if you see somebody in trouble, and you know that they have done nothing wrong, you should always try to help them, even if they were a dragon! Secondly, just because somebody is an angry looking person, it doesn't mean that they are horrible. They are just like everybody else, and like everybody else they need good friends in their life. So you should always try to be a friend, and appreciate them when they do something for you.

George and the Dragon had grown to be very good friends. Seref was happy to have him as a friend because he had saved his life, and George was happy because Seref had never forgotten what he had done for him, and this had made their friendship everlasting.

The end.

Chapter 1

Up in the highlands of Scotland there is a loch called Ness. This loch is very much like a lake, however this is a very special Loch. It is bigger than all the lakes in England, Scotland and Wales put together, the largest in the land and is more than 22 miles long and over 750 feet deep. Many people from all over the world would go to this Loch Ness for a chance to see the monster that lives there, the Loch Ness Monster! Some people would say the stories were made up, but many people still believed it was true, because they had seen it for themselves. They say that it looks like a dinosaur. The local people did not have a problem with a monster living in the loch, as they even gave it a name, and so has it had become affectionately known as Nessie.

Nessie was rarely seen. Did this mean Nessie was shy? Every

year many people go to this loch to see if they can see the monster, but every year they would leave disappointed because they had not managed to get even a glimpse. If only they could see her one-day, they could prove she is real.

One such group to visit the loch was a party of students from a school in Scotland. A local named Glyn, a highlander born and bred, was their tour guide, and the students were accompanied by their teacher Matt. As Glyn showed them around the loch, the students were messing about and not paying attention to their tour. All except one young boy called Sam, who was paying close attention to the loch, looking keenly through his binoculars. Sam was determined to try his hardest to spot Nessie. He was a creative boy, and felt that he might be able to find Nessie where others had not looked. Whilst he was searching, his friends Lisa, Martin, Jade and Steve were teasing their teacher and being naughty. If they didn't pay attention, they would surely miss the chance to see Nessie.

Chapter 2

The day was nearing the end, and the tour was almost over. Sam still hadn't spotted Nessie, and it was getting dark. Had he missed her? He was sure he had looked everywhere! As the group began to walk away towards their mini-bus, Sam stayed behind, patiently waiting by the jetty on the edge of the loch. Glyn noticed what Sam was doing, and stayed back with him...staring out into the black waters with a wise old twinkle in his eye, and just then "NO WAY!" shouted out Sam. He moved his binoculars and brought them back to his eyes again, checking whether he was seeing this for real or whether it was his equipment. By now Sam was trembling with excitement! What had he seen? He excitedly looked around for his group, but they were all to far away, there be only a smiling Glyn. The man knew what Sam had seen. Peering through the lens, Sam saw Nessie giggling back at him! She's wearing a disguise? No wonder why people could not find her! Nessie was tricking the visitors...how cheeky thought Sam. Then, as quickly as she'd appeared...WHOOSH! And she was gone. Sam turned to Glyn, "did you know Nessie wore a disguise?" he asked. Glyn gave a wry smile, "Oh aye, ole Nessay is a wee bit of a trickster. I'd like to see anyone believe that one! Now off you go, you don't want to be left behind!"

Sam ran back to the van in excitement, he couldn't wait to tell the rest of the group. "I saw her, I SAW NESSIE!" he shouted as her ran towards the mini-van. As he got into the van, the rest of the group just laughed at him. "Yea, yea … of course you did Sam!" It didn't make a difference, and Sam didn't care, he knew what he'd saw and he would be back to see her again!

Chapter 3

The weekend had arrived, and it was the day that Sam had waited all week for. He would be going back to Loch Ness! It would be a long train journey to Inverness, where the loch was, so Sam could not go alone! That wasn't going to stop him

though, because he had someone by his side. All week, at school and in his house, he had tried to tell everyone what he'd saw, but nobody had believed him, nobody except for Nicole, his older sister. Nicole was the coolest older sister ever, as not only did she believe her younger brother, she was also happy to go with him so that he could have another chance at finding Nessie.

Sam thought all week about what he'd seen. He just couldn't forget the image of Nessie wearing the disguise. Where on earth did she even get it? Did she wear it so she couldn't be recognised? It was odd enough that there was a large monster living in a loch, let alone one that knew how to prank! Nessie certainly had a sense of humour. Sam also wandered how much Glyn the guide knew. Were they in the joke together? There were so many questions that needed to be answered, and Sam was on a mission to answer them all.

Nicole and Sam arrived at Inverness station, and asked the taxi driver to take them to Loch Ness. They were both so very excited, as they got closer and closer to their destination. As they approached the loch, Sam spotted Glyn standing on the jetty at the edge of the loch, exactly where they had been earlier in the week. They paid the taxi driver and ran over to where Glyn was standing. "I told you I'd be back!" said Sam.

"Aye, never doubted it lad!" replied Glyn. "How could you not after what you saw? Ahh, and who is this bonnie lass then eh?" "Hi, I'm Nicole...I am Sam's sister." "So I see you also had to see for yourself aye?" asked Glyn. "How could I not, this is a once in a lifetime opportunity!" replied Nicole.

As they were speaking there was an almighty CRASH that was louder than thunder! "Whoa...what was that?" cried out Sam. Nicole stood frozen in shock, and even Glyn looked confused! As they looked around, they saw that a boat had crashed into the rock face! "How on earth did that happen?!" shouted out Glyn. The boat would surely start to sink, how would they save the people on board?

"Quickly, come with me" shouted Glyn, as he raced towards his boat. Nicole and Sam looked at each other and they both knew that it was down to them to save the people on the boat. They jumped on board, and Glyn furiously tried to start up the motor. It wasn't working. Meanwhile, Sam was looking through his binoculars, and could see the ship starting to sink. Beside the ship was Nessie! Sam couldn't believe it, was she going to eat the people? He couldn't tell because Nessie was still wearing the silly disguise. Suddenly, the boat's motor roared into life. Glyn put the motor in full speed as they headed towards the sinking boat. As they got closer, Nessie disappeared into the depths of the loch. Nicole and Sam threw the life floats into the water, luckily there had only been 3 people in the boat, and so they just had enough to save them!

Nicole, Sam and Glyn were heroes! They had helped to save the boat crews' lives. However, it was a mystery as to how the boat had crashed in the first place. "One moment we were nice and steady, and in the next moment the boat just flipped over!" said the Captain in his thick Scottish accent. Everybody

was confused, but not Glyn. He was sure he knew what had happened. Can you guess what it was?

As the Captain and his crew left, they thanked Nicole, Sam and Glyn. There were just the three of them left, right back where they had started. Now that they were alone, Glyn reached into his coat pocket and pulled out a funny looking whistle. He then went to his boat to collect an umbrella. He opened the umbrella and began to blow into the whistle, but no sound came from it! Nicole and Sam began to laugh, "it doesn't even work!" cried out Sam. He was laughing so much that his belly began to ache, as Glyn kept on blowing his silent whistle. At that moment…"SPLASH!" A huge wave of water landed on Nicole and Sam, and out of the water came Nessie! The water had soaked them both, now they were definitely not laughing, this time it was Nessie and Glyn! "Ha-ha-ha!" roared Glyn, he laughed so much his belly began to shake! Of course he had nown that this would happen. Just then, he stopped, and turned to Nessie, Glyn did not look happy! "You have been a very, very naughty girl, Nessie!" said Glyn. "How many times have I told you not to play dangerously with people? Those men could have been hurt! Why did you do that Nessie?" asked Glyn. Nessie whimpered, she didn't like being in trouble. "I was only playing Glyn" she replied. After hearing her speak, Nicole almost fainted! She had never seen a speaking sea monster before! "I was pretending to be in trouble, and when the nice men came to help me, and then I flipped over the boat, I didn't know it would crash into the rocks, I'm so sorry!"

Glyn crossed his arms, as he was not happy with Nessie. At that moment, Sam remembered something Nicole had said taught him when he was just a little boy, and thought this advice could help Nessie. "Thank you for telling the truth Nessie" he said. "It's perfectly fine to have fun, I do it too, but you don't want to 'cry wolf' because people will stop believing you!" Nessie looked confused, "what does that mean?" she asked. Sam smiled and explained, "if you pretend you are in trouble, and people come to help but find out you were only joking, they will be less likely to help you the next time you cry for help when you really need it." Nessie thought for a moment, and nodded. She had understood, and smiled because it made sense to her. Does it make sense to you? Nicole looked proudly at Sam, she couldn't believe he had remembered and understood the lesson she had taught him. Glyn could see that Nessie was sorry and she had learnt this important lesson, and was no longer angry, he knew she would change for the better. However, this was still Nessie, a cheeky and fun loving creature. With a quick flick of her tail, she crashed it into the water making a huge wave that soaked them all again, including Glyn! They all laughed, and as Nessie swam away she said, "I'll never forget what you've told me Sam, and please come back so we can play another day!"

The end.
(Until the next adventures!)